LITTLE "b" MAKES A BUNNY,
LITTLE "d" MAKES A DUCKY

ISBN: 978-1-0878-5693-3

LITTLE "b" MAKES A BUNNY, LITTLE "d" MAKES A DUCKY

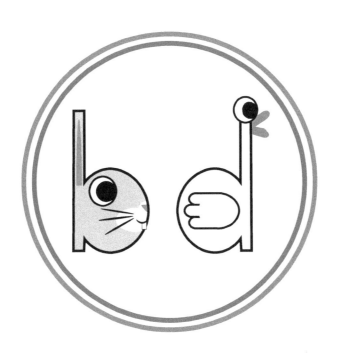

STORY AND ILLUSTRATIONS
BY HEATHER M. THOMPSON

Little-"b"-Bunny:
A bunny made with
little "b".

Little-"d"-Ducky:
A ducky made with
little "d".

These are the characters in this book.
Let's learn about them. Let's take a look!

Which little letter is this?

Which little letter is this?

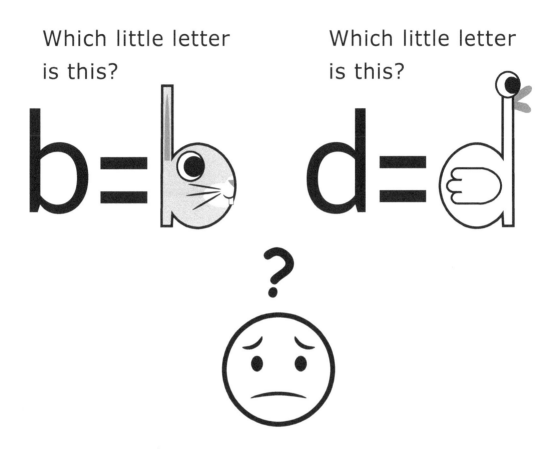

Sometimes confused. Sometimes mixed up. No need to worry. We'll get that fixed up!

I have tall ears that
do not flop.

A round face
for whiskers.

Now hop!

I'm in reverse,
starting in back.

A round
body.

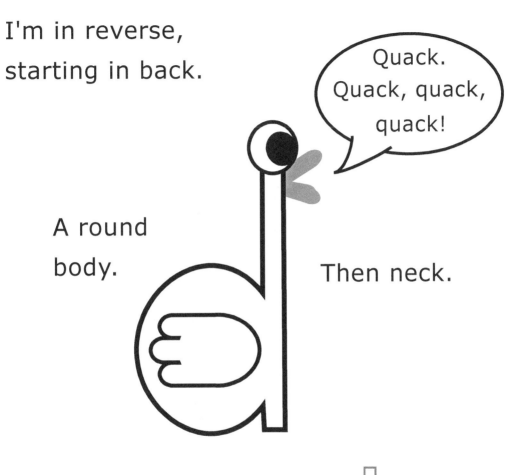

Then neck.

Now quack!

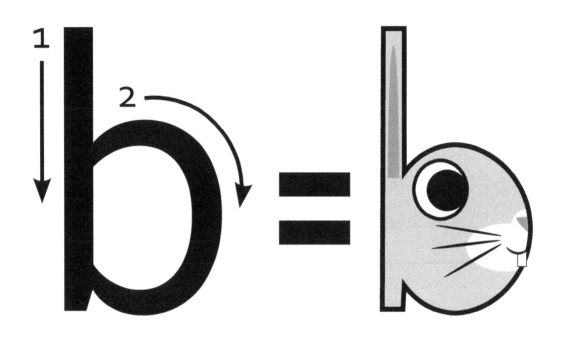

A line then circle makes little "b". Now turn it into a hopping bunny!

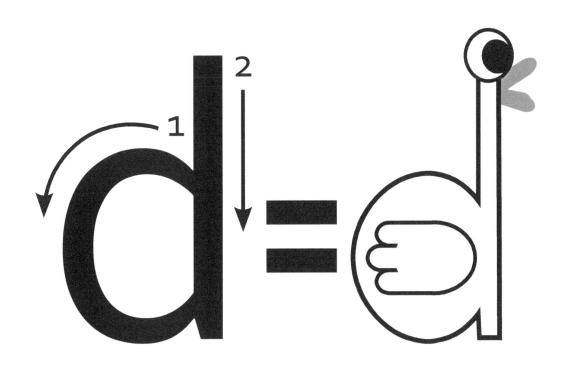

A circle then line makes little "d". Now turn it into a quacking ducky!

Little-"b"-Bunny. Little-"d"-Ducky. Our "b" and "d" friends. They tell us, is it line or circle how little "b" or little "d" ends?

Let's read with our friends. Let's read a little more. They have a small quest. Something to explore.

Our bunny likes "b" words. For ducks, "d" words are better. What words can we find that start with each letter?

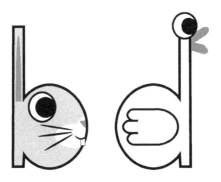

b

banana

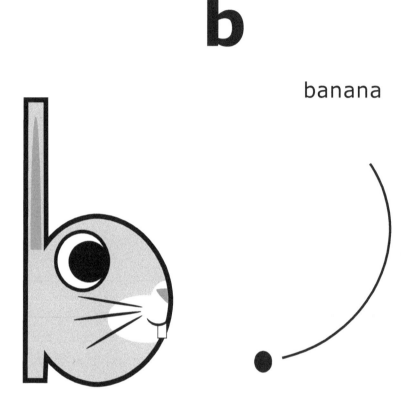

Little-"b"-Bunny eats a banana for breakfast. Nutritious!

d

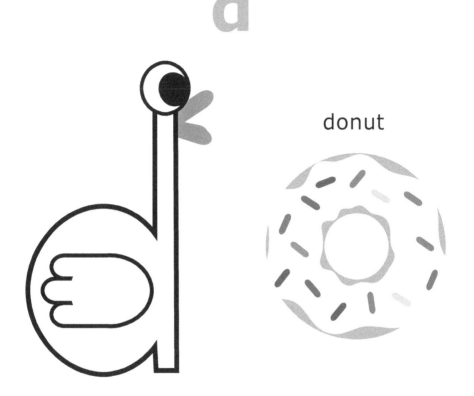

donut

Little-"d"-Ducky eats a donut for dinner.
Delicious!

b

blue bow

Little-"b"-Bunny pins a blue bow on her ear.

d

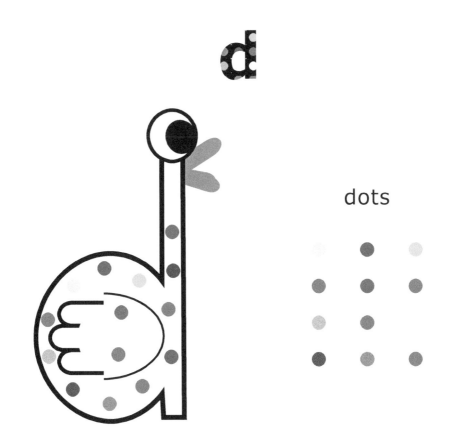

dots

Little-"d"-Ducky dresses in dots.
Oh, dear!

bus

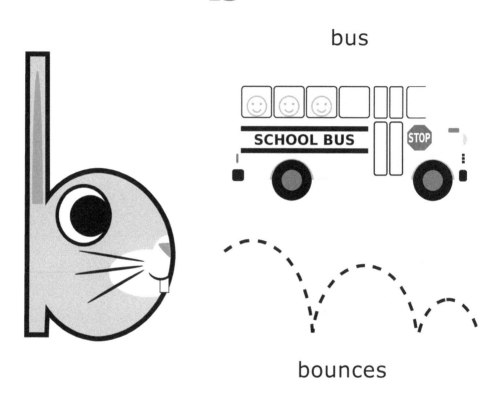

bounces

Little-"b"-Bunny bounces. She finds it more fun than taking a bus.

dances

Little-"d"-Ducky dances to music while quacking at us.

b

butterfly

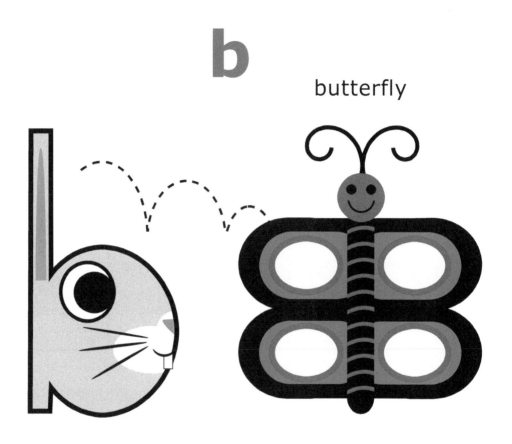

Little-"b"-Bunny hops behind a butterfly made with big "B"!

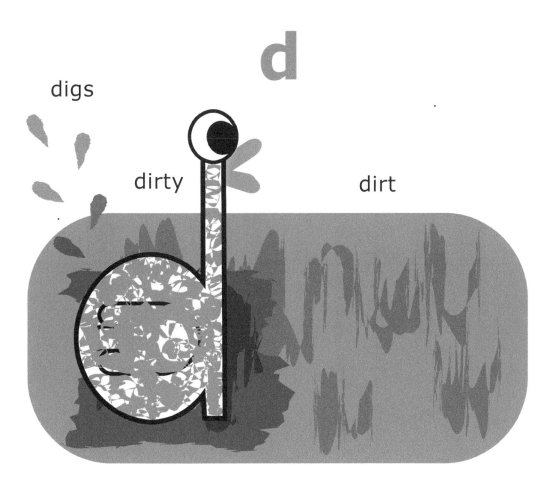

Little-"d"-Ducky digs deep in the dirt and gets VERY dirty.

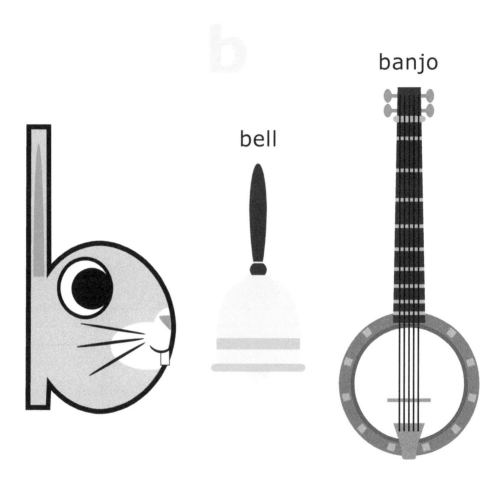

Little-"b"-Bunny plays in a band -- the bell and banjo, too.

d

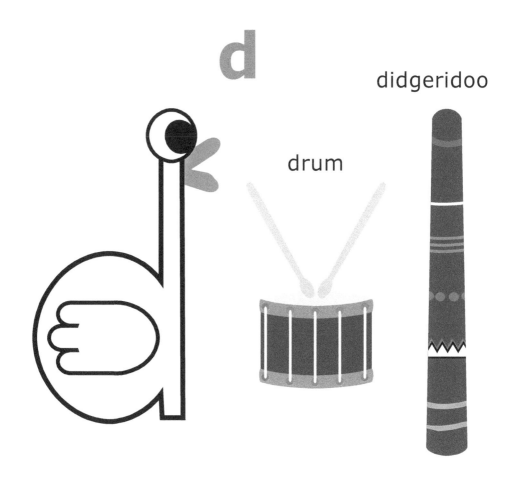

didgeridoo

drum

Little-"d"-Ducky joins in with a drum and a didgeridoo!

b

bear

blocks

ball

Little-"b"-Bunny's Toys

black bag

Little-"b"-Bunny puts her bear, blocks, and ball in a black bag.

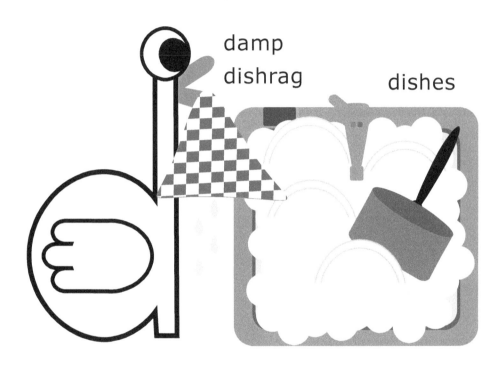

damp dishrag

dishes

Little-"d"-Ducky does the dishes with a damp dishrag.

b e d

It's the end of the day. All has gone well.
Both go to bed. And look what they spell!

We've finished our book. Yes, it is done. Our little letter friends do hope you had fun! Just one final thing they would like you to see, some words that begin with little "b" or little "d".

b

bunny   banana   bus   bell   black

book   breakfast   behind   banjo   bag

back   blue   butterfly   bear   both

body   bow   big   blocks   bed

better   bounces   band   ball   begin

d

ducky   dresses   deep   didgeridoo

ducks   dots   dirt   does   day

donut   dear   dirty   dishes   done

dinner   dances   drum   damp   do

delicious   digs   dishrag

Lightning Source UK Ltd.
Milton Keynes UK
UKHW050747140622
404398UK00003B/25

9 781087 856933